The Farmer

XIMO ABADIA

Holiday House · New York

In the village,
everyone is resting.

Not Paul.
Paul mows.

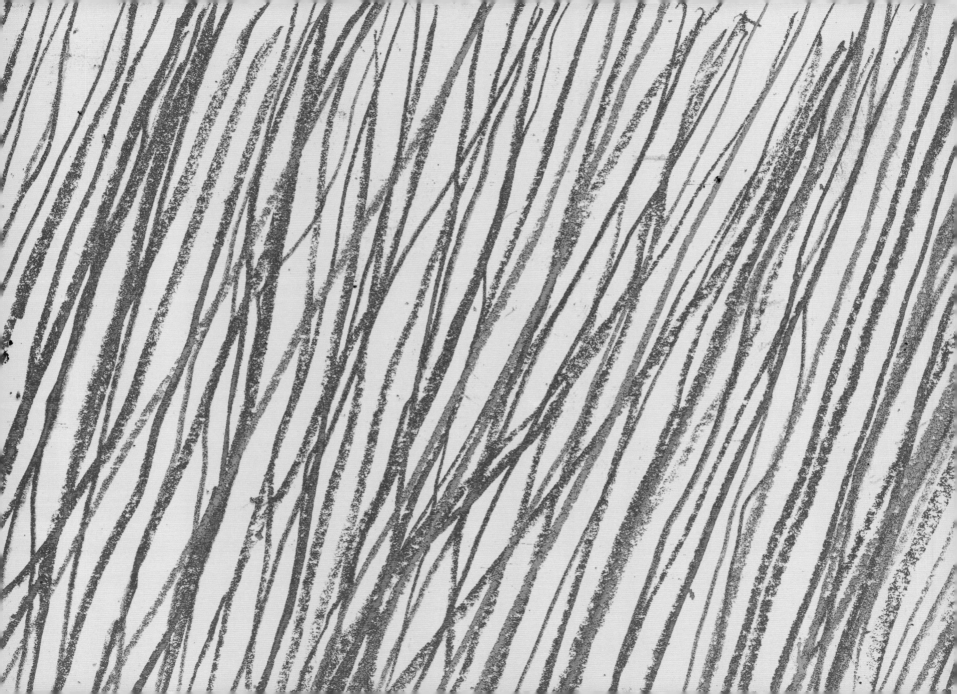

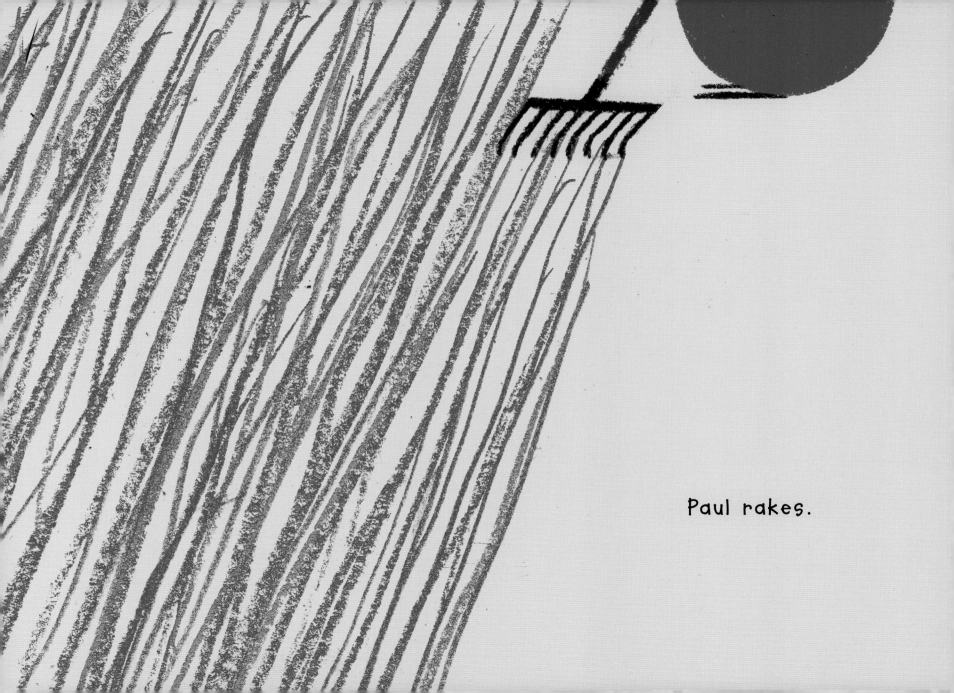

Paul rakes.

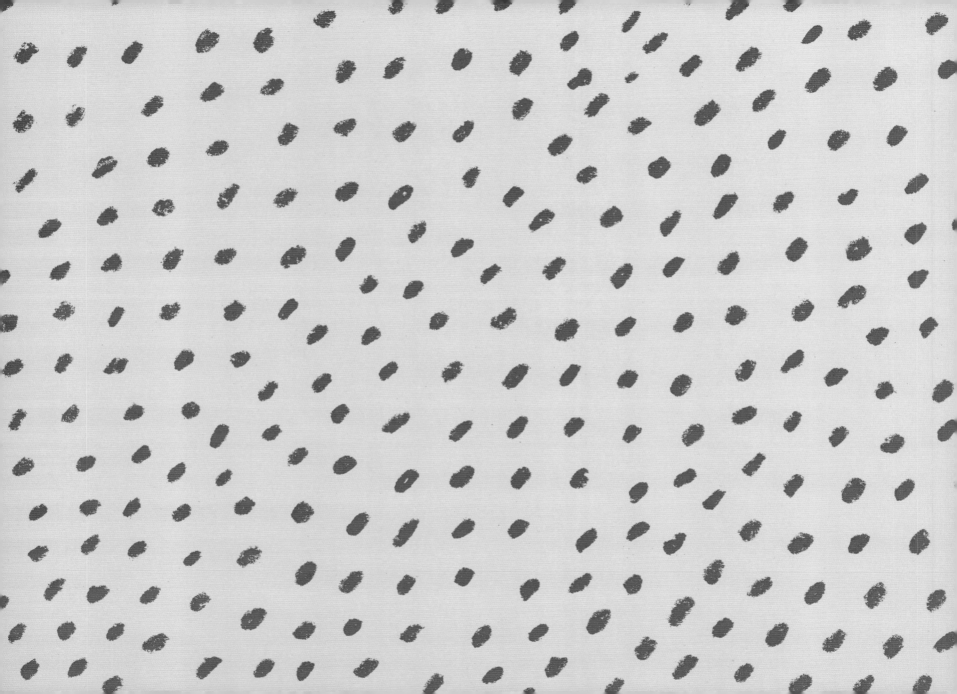

Paul digs.

Paul draws water . . .

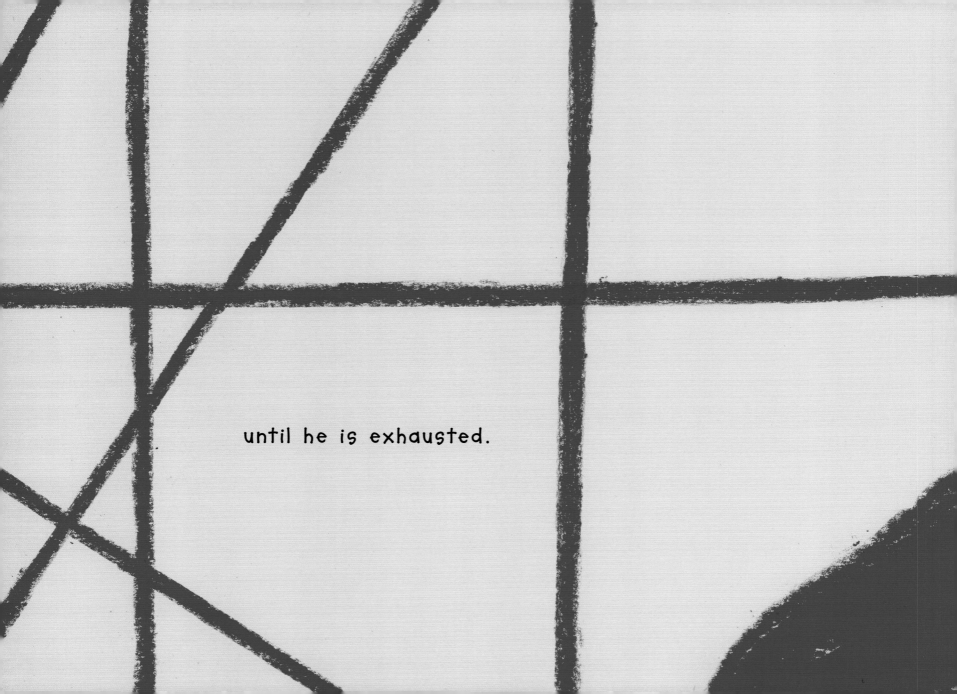

until he is exhausted.

Every day, Paul watches, inspects, checks.

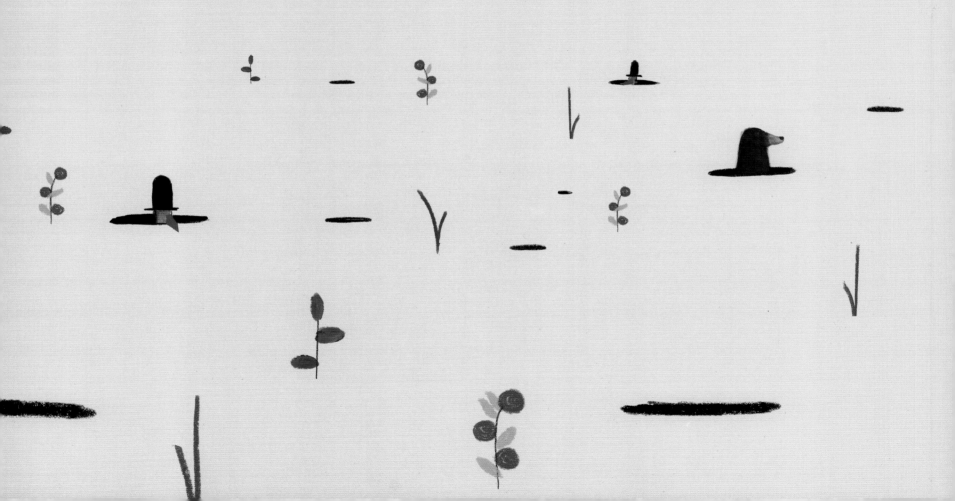

Finally, everything begins
to grow.

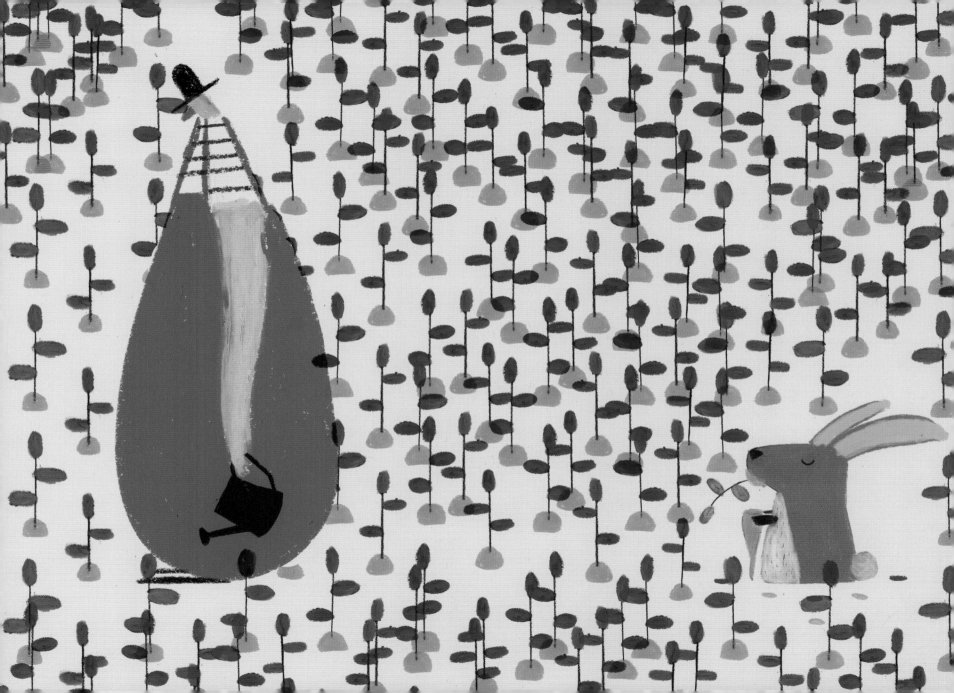

Then . . . everything becomes dry.

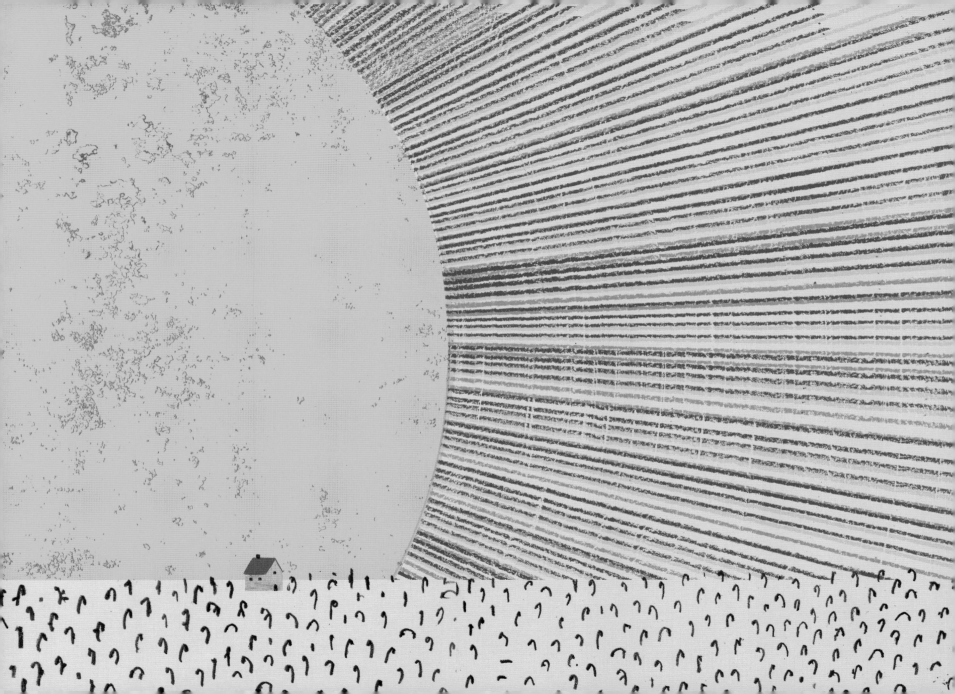

There is not one drop of
water for Paul's plants.
Paul despairs.

But Paul is not alone . . .

and his
friend the rain
is never truly
far away.

Library of Congress Cataloging-in-Publication Data

Names: Abadia, Ximo, 1983- author, illustrator. | Maccarone, Grace, translator. | Loughman, Kelly, translator.
Title: The farmer / Ximo Abadia ; English translation by Grace Maccarone and Kelly Loughman.
Other titles: Potager. English
Description: First edition. | New York : Holiday House, 2019.
Originally published: Geneva, Switzerland : Editions La Joie de lire S.A., 2017 under the title Le potager.
Summary: Paul works hard on his farm while those in the village are resting, but when drought comes,
friends unexpectedly arrive to lend a hand.
Identifiers: LCCN 2018019137 | ISBN 9780823441587 (hardcover)
Subjects: | CYAC: Farm life—Fiction. | Drought—Fiction. | Helpfulness—Fiction. | Animals—Fiction.
Classification: LCC PZ7.1.A15 Far 2019 | DDC [E]—dc23 LC record available at https://lccn.loc.gov/2018019137

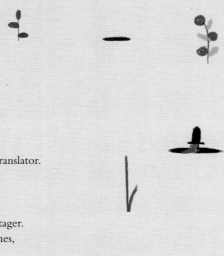